The
Day They
Left the Bay

The Day They Left the Bay

By Mick Blackistone
Illustrated by Lee Boynton

BLUE CRAB PRESS
ANNAPOLIS, M.D.

Printed in Mexico
First Printing 1988 Acropolis Books Ltd.
Second Printing 1991 Blue Crab Press
Third Printing 1995 Blue Crab Press
Fourth Printing 1997 Blue Crab Press
Fifth Printing 2003 Blue Crab Press
ISBN 0-9627726-3-1

Library of Congress Catalog Card Number 91-076591
Copyright 1991 by Blue Crab Press
P.O. Box 67, Tracys Landing, MD 20779

The Chesapeake Bay

The Chesapeake Bay is the largest estuary in North America. An estuary is a semi-enclosed body of water where an ocean or sea joins with a river or other source of water that drains from land. Since oceans are full of salt water, while rivers flow with fresh water, the two meeting in an estuary such as the Chesapeake Bay blend into a measurable mixture of mildly salty water called brackish water.

The Chesapeake Bay is 185 miles long and ranges from 3 to 22 miles in width. The average depth is only 21 feet, but it reaches 174 feet at the deepest spot, a place called Bloody Point off the southern end of Kent Island. A total of 46 principal rivers flow into the Bay, draining an area of about 64,000 miles that includes parts of Maryland, Virginia, Delaware, Pennsylvania, and New York.

Maryland owns more Chesapeake Bay shoreline than any of the other states. Seventeen Maryland counties and the city of Baltimore border upon the tidal water of the Chesapeake, 123 miles of the Bay's total length and 4,100 miles of shoreline in all. Of the many different types of tidewater plants found in the region of the Chesapeake Bay, one of the richest bodies of water in the world, many grow in Maryland's 350,000 acres of tidal wetlands. These plants or "food factories" provide basic fare for tiny animals that in turn are consumed by larger species. This is called the "food chain." The valuable species of shell and fin fish, oysters, clams, crabs, shad, rock, perch and other, are included in this chain. At the top of the chain is man.

Dedicated to the Chesapeake Bay
of today and the children of tomorrow,
and to all people working to preserve the
environmental integrity of our national
waterways, coastlines, and lakes.

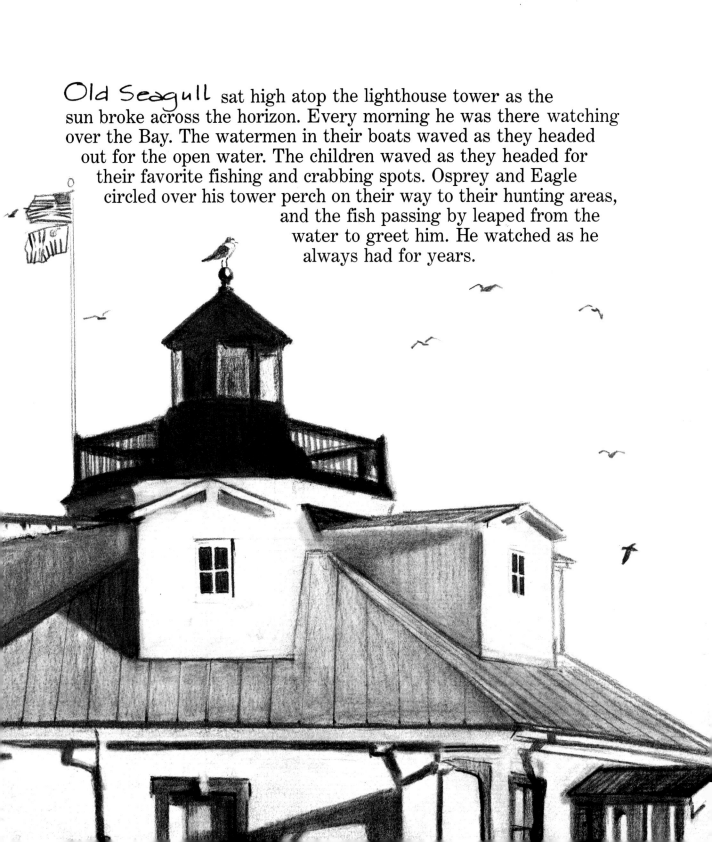

Old Seagull sat high atop the lighthouse tower as the sun broke across the horizon. Every morning he was there watching over the Bay. The watermen in their boats waved as they headed out for the open water. The children waved as they headed for their favorite fishing and crabbing spots. Osprey and Eagle circled over his tower perch on their way to their hunting areas, and the fish passing by leaped from the water to greet him. He watched as he always had for years.

As the spring and early summer days passed, Old Seagull noticed that the watermen and children did not seem as happy when they want out on the Bay in the morning. Osprey and Eagle were often gone much longer on their hunting trips...often coming back without food. Days would go by before Old Seagull saw a school of fish, and when he did see one, it was a small group. He continued to watch as he always had for years.

Old Seagull watched...

and waited....

One day in the middle of the summer, he sensed there really was a great sadness in all the creatures above and below his lighthouse tower perch. And it was time, after all these years, to do something he had never done before. It was time for action. With the driving motion of his powerful wings, he left his lighthouse tower and soared to the hunting area of Osprey and Eagle.

Soon he reached a channel marker that was a resting spot for Osprey. Gliding down on the wind, he stared straight into the eyes of the hunter. Osprey was surprised to see Old Seagull, but did not move as the Grandfather of the Bay came closer.

"Why have you left your tower perch and come to my hunting grounds?" asked Osprey.

"I feel a great sadness," Old Seagull said. "Come to the lighthouse at the end of the day, and I will talk with you then." With those words, he caught a wind shift and soared upwards into the clouds in search of Eagle.

In a while, he came upon a small creek that
emptied into the great Bay. Searching the trees along
the shore, he spotted the eagle resting on a branch
near the top of the largest pine. He flew closer.
Mighty Eagle had never had the honor of a visit
from the Grandfather of the Bay, and did not move
as Old Seagull circled slowly overhead.
"Why have you left your tower
perch and come to my hunting ground,
Grandfather?" Eagle asked.
"I feel a great sadness,"
Old Seagull said. "Come to the
lighthouse at the end of the
day, and I will talk with you
then." With those words he
caught a wind shift and soared
downwind in search of Bluefish.

An hour passed. He continued looking below the surface of the water for the fish coming from the great ocean. Finally, far ahead, he spotted a rippling on the water. As he glided closer and hovered a few feet above the water, a large Bluefish broke the surface.

"Why have you come to see us, Grandfather?" asked Bluefish as other fish swam in all directions around him.

"I feel a great sadness," Old Seagull said. "Come to the lighthouse at the end of the day, and I will talk with you then." With those words he caught a wind shift and soared towards his lighthouse tower home.

Upon reaching the lighthouse tower, Old Seagull rested and watched as he had done for years. Late in the afternoon, as the first workboat passed by the tower heading for home port, he noticed that none of the men waved as they passed. As the children returned from their fishing spots in an old rowboat, they were quiet and didn't look up at his perch. There was great sadness. He also noticed that the sun was beginning to hide itself behind the treeline on the western horizon. Soon Osprey, Eagle, and Bluefish would arrive.

First to reach the lighthouse was Osprey. He had the shortest distance to travel from his hunting grounds. He remained silent when he landed on the huge rock at the base of the lighthouse. He knew from his father before him that he must always place himself below Old Seagull and that he should not speak unless Old Seagull

spoke to him. Osprey knew that he should be patient and wait silently for Old Seagull to speak.

Eagle and Bluefish arrived moments later. Eagle landed next to Osprey, and Bluefish stopped a few feet beneath the surface at the foot of the lighthouse. They, too, waited patiently and silently for the time when Old Seagull was ready to speak.

At last, Old Seagull left his tower perch and flew to a rock at the base of the lighthouse. All listened as Grandfather spoke.

"You are the Eagle whom I have called because you talk to the animals of the land near the Bay. You are the Bluefish whom I have called because you know the fish, crabs, clams, and other creatures from beneath the waters. You are the Osprey, who lives both on the land and on the water, and you travel far and wide across our homeland," said Old Seagull.

"I sense there is a sadness," he continued, "as I watch the people going by on their boats. I watch you, my friends, return from your hunting grounds without food. This is not as it should be. The Bay is our home and has always given us food, shelter and a place to teach our young our ways of life. We have lived happily with each other and with people for hundreds of years."

"I agree," said Eagle. "We, the animals on land, are sad because the Bay is sick and our food is disappearing. Even the people in their boats are sad. There are many reasons for us to worry."

Bluefish listened and said, "I, too, agree with you. Things are very bad here. The water is dirty. There is not enough oxygen in it for us to breathe. We cannot stay in the Bay. We must swim somewhere else or die. The fish live and feed the Eagle, the Osprey and man. But, if the Bay cannot feed us, then we cannot feed the birds or man either, Grandfather."

I have watched our children leaving and our fellow animals, fish, and birds dying," said Old Seagull. "Osprey, you are a traveler. Do you agree?"

"Yes, I, too, sense this sadness. I want to live the way we have always lived...animals side by side, and with people too. But now the Ospreys are sad and our young ones are hungry. You, Grandfather, must decide what must be done."

The Old Seagull sat quietly for a moment, reflecting on what his friends had said.

"It is true that many things in the Bay must change. We must hope that the people who have helped us all many times before will make their brothers and sisters help us and the Bay now. We need these changes if we, the Bay creatures, are to raise our young here and continue to live happily with man. But, my friends, can the Bay become strong again?" questioned Old Seagull.

"I could give the people many ideas," interrupted Osprey angrily.

They should stop throwing trash into our creeks and waterways. They should stop poisoning the water from their businesses and lawns. They should stop farm fertilizer and soil from washing into the Bay with the rainwater. They should stop the dirt that washes into the water from construction sites and roads near the water's edge. Boaters should not throw trash—especially plastic soda-can collars—into the water. Oh, I could tell them many things to do."

"We must be strong in what we do and say," said Eagle. "The people must learn that by doing those things Osprey talked about, they are not only hurting our children, but their children, too. If the human children learned these things now, they would grow to be kind to our children. Then the Bay would become well again. Our brothers and sisters will become strong and live in greater numbers as they did when you were young, Grandfather."

"But what do we do now?" asked Bluefish.

Old Seagull listened patiently before he spoke. "We will do what has never been done before," he said. "We will leave our homes in the water, on the land, and in the trees. You, all of you, will gather your brothers, sisters and young ones. We will all leave the Bay until the lessons are learned.

"But, we can't leave. Where will we go?" asked Eagle.

"I will lead you," said Old Seagull. "You will pass my words on. Three nights from now, when the moon is full, all of the Bay creatures in the water, on the land, and in the air will leave. I have spoken."

For the next two days
Old Seagull sat high atop his lighthouse
tower, watching the watermen going out
onto the Bay and the young children
going into the creeks to fish and crab.
There was sadness in their eyes. They
returned home at the end of each day
with few fish and fewer crabs.

HIGH VOLTAGE
CABLE CROSSING
DO NOT ANCHOR

On the third night, as the moon shone brightly, shadows of animals, fish, and birds by the hundreds filed from their homes past the lighthouse tower and Old Seagull.

As Eagle approached the tower, he called to Old Seagull, "Grandfather, we need you now. Our brothers and sisters are moving quickly from their homes and you must lead them."

With that, the mighty seagull rose from the tower, caught in a light breeze, and glided down the Bay.

The next morning as the sun began to break across the horizon, the workboats appeared through the mist heading for the lighthouse and the open Bay. As the watermen went by the lighthouse, one glanced up at the tower and noticed that the old seagulll that had been there for years was gone. With little thought, except that it was strange seeing the tower without the old bird, he cruised on.

When the boats returned that evening, there was a greater sadness than ever before in the men's hearts because not one fish or crab was caught. The children, too, came home complaining to their parents that they hadn't caught anything all day. And so it was to be the next day, and the next.

A week later, the people began talking to each other, only to find out that no one had seen any Bay creatures in the water, in the woods, or in the air. They went to the town leaders and to the newspapers, but no one knew anything about where the Bay creatures had gone. And, so it was to be, day after day.

Then one day an old workboat came slowly up the Bay into the largest town's harbor.

As the workboat pulled up to the dock, an old man with a twinkle in his eye and faded clothing stepped on to the pier and tied lines to two pilings.

"Nothing out there to catch," said a boy sitting on the bulkhead. "There are no fish, no crabs, no oysters, no birds, no wild animals. There are no Bay animals anywhere, and we are really sad."

"I know," said the old man. "But I am going to tell you how to get them back. Come over here and sit with me while I tell you what to do."

As the old man with the twinkle in his eye spoke, the boy sat and silently listened to every word. The old man told him to tell the newspapers and magazines and town leaders that the people had to stop throwing trash into the creeks and waterways. The businesses had to stop the poisons from going into the water. Cities and towns had to improve their sewage treatment. Farmers had to save their fertilizer and their soil. The builders had to stop the dirt from going into the creeks and rivers and had to stop cutting down so many trees from their land. When the old man had told the boy the many things people should do, he said with a twinkle in his eye, "Tell everyone that people can't take from the Bay more than the Bay can give to them."

"They won't believe me! I'm only a kid!" said the boy.

"They might not *want* to believe you. But you must make them believe you," said the old man with a twinkle in his eye. "They will listen, and when the people start doing what needs to be done, the animals, the fish, and the birds will return, and everyone will be happy once again."

With that the old man slowly boarded his old workboat, untied the lines and cast off.

"Hey, where are you going?" called the boy. "Aren't you staying to help me?"

"No," said the old man. "It's in your hands now. You tell them what must be done." And he quietly slipped out of the harbor.

As the boy stood on the dock, he thought about how sad everyone was at not seeing any birds circling overhead looking for food in the harbor water.

Suddenly, he ran toward the town newspaper office to tell "his story."

At the newspaper office the reporters and editor listened curiously. Finally, the editor agreed with the boy that "we must convince people to stop talking and start cleaning up the Bay." He assigned reporters to begin working on the story. Reaching all the people of the Bay area would take a lot of hard work, but the newspaper would tell "the story."

"I must go to the town leaders, too," said the boy. "They must get all the leaders in all the towns to tell the people."

"I know the mayor," said the newspaper editor. "Come with me, and we will go together."

At City Hall the boy and the newspaper editor had a long talk with the mayor of the town. The boy told the story of the old man and what had to happen if things were going to get better for the Bay and if people were going to be happy again. The mayor agreed and said that he would talk to the leaders of all the other towns.

There were many things that had to be done, and environmentalists, scientists, and educators worked to put their information into the hands of all the people...young and old. People who lived many miles from the water had to help protect the Bay, too. Rain washing chemicals, poisons, and waste from their homes into streams carried these deadly substances into creeks and rivers, and eventually into the great Bay.

Watermen who worked on the water told the people that their pollution and building of homes near the water had made it difficult for sea life to live. Over the years, the Bay grasses had disappeared and oyster, fish, and crab harvests had declined, and it was harder and harder to earn a living to support their families.

As the days went by, word spread that people needed to start cleaning up the Bay. Newspapers and environmentalists told them how to help. While some people grumbled about the hard work that was needed, more and more children and adults forgot about their sadness and began to work very hard to make the Bay better.

Children and their parents set out in their boats and joined the workmen in pulling trash from all the creeks and waterways. Large, flat barges were placed at the heads of major creeks, and as trash was collected by the small boats, the people piled it on the barge to be taken to the shore for dump trucks to haul away. The people

were shocked by the great numbers of old tires, televisions, refrigerators, and car parts that had been thrown in the creeks and Bay over the years. They put trash cans near the water with signs that said, "Put Your Trash Here—Not In The Water!" The farmers began to fertilize and plow their fields differently, and the businesses began to watch very closely what chemicals went from their factories into the Bay. The cities and towns set to work to improve the way their sewage treatment plants worked. The builders started to leave the trees up and began building houses farther from the water. Families found ways to reduce their household wastes and reduced the fertilizers they put on their lawns. Many changes were taking place and the people felt happier in their hearts.

Everyone in the Bay area helped a little every day. As the weeks and months went by, many changes took place. The boy felt very glad and was very proud of all the people.

Months later, one Spring morning, as the sun began to creep up over the horizon and the marsh mist began to rise, the watermen headed out from their docks...not to fish or crab, but to continue their Bay clean-up work. As the first boat reached the lighthouse, a waterman looked toward the lighthouse tower perch that had been empty for so many months. Up on his perch was the Old Seagull. He watched as he always had for years.

At the sight of the Old Seagull, the waterman gave out a cry of happiness and others drew near to look at the great bird again. They too, were overcome with joy because all their hard work had finally brought back the creatures of the Bay.

Off in the marsh mist sat a workboat silently drifting.
An old man with a twinkle in his eye watched
with gladness
in his heart.